Vaughn

This edition copyright © by Wieser & Wieser, Inc.
and Richard Horner Associates, 1990.

This edition published in 1990 by Gallery Books,
an imprint of W. H. Smith Publishers, Inc.,
112 Madison Avenue, New York, NY 10016.

Gallery Books are available for bulk purchase for sales
promotions and premium use. For details write or telephone
Manager of Special Sales, W. H. Smith Publishers, Inc.,
112 Madison Avenue, New York, NY 10016. (212) 532-6600

Illustrations copyright © by Berta and Elmer Hader, 1937.

ISBN 0-8317-42747

Printed in Hong Kong

A VISIT FROM ST. NICHOLAS

BY
CLEMENT C. MOORE

ILLUSTRATED BY
BERTA ✝ ELMER HADER

North Pole

1
Santa Claus

GALLERY BOOKS

'Twas the night before
Christmas,
when all
through
the
house

Not a creature was
stirring,
not even
a
mouse!

The stockings were hung by
the chimney with care,
In hopes that St. Nicholas
soon would be there.

The children were nestled
all snug in their beds,
While visions of sugarplums
danced in their heads.

And Mamma in her kerchief,
and I in my cap,
Had just settled our brains for
a long winter's nap—

When out on the lawn there
arose such a clatter,
I sprang from my bed to see
what was the matter.

Away to the window I flew
  like a flash,
Tore open the shutters and
  threw up the sash.

The moon on the breast of
  the new-fallen snow
Gave a luster of midday
  to objects below,

When what to my wondering
   eyes should appear,
But—
   a miniature sleigh
and eight tiny reindeer,

With a little old driver so lively
   and quick
I knew in a moment it must
   be St. Nick!

More rapid than eagles his
coursers they came,
And he whistled and shouted
and called them by name:

"Now, Dasher! Now, Dancer!
Now, Prancer and Vixen!
On, Comet! On, Cupid! On,
Donder and Blitzen!

"To the top of the porch, to the
top of the wall!
Now, dash away, dash away,
dash away all!"

As dry leaves that before the wild
    hurricane fly,
When they meet with an
    obstacle, mount to the sky,
So up to the housetop the
    coursers they flew,

With the sleigh full of toys—
and St. Nicholas, too.
And then in a twinkling I
heard on the roof,
The prancing and pawing
of each little hoof.

As I drew in my head, and
was turning around,
Down the chimney St. Nicholas
came with a bound.

He was dressed all in fur
  from his head to his foot,
And his clothes were all
  tarnished with ashes and soot.

A bundle of toys he had
  flung on his back,
And he looked like a peddler
  just opening his pack.

His eyes—how they twinkled!
  His dimples—how merry!
His cheeks were like roses,
  his nose like a cherry.

His droll little mouth was
drawn up like a bow,
And the beard on his chin
was as white as the snow.

The stump of a pipe he held
tight in his teeth,
And the smoke it encircled
his head like a wreath.

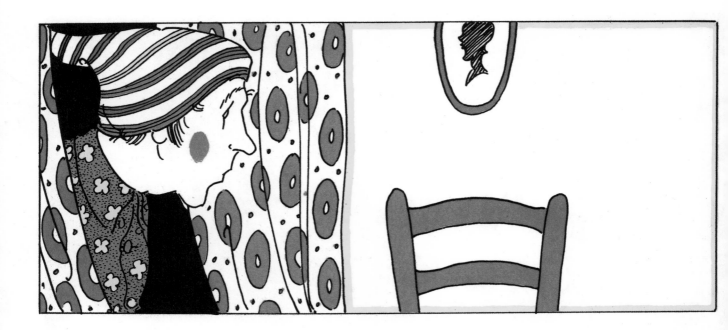

He had a broad face and a little
  round belly
That shook, when he laughed,
  like a bowlful of jelly.

He was chubby and plump—a
  right jolly old elf,
And I laughed when I saw him,
  in spite of myself.

A wink of his eye and a twist
of his head
Soon gave me to know I had
nothing to dread.

He spoke not a word,
    but went straight to his work,
And filled all the stockings—

then turned with a jerk,
And laying his finger aside
of his nose,
And giving a nod—

Up
  the
    chimney
     he
      rose!

He sprang to his sleigh,
  to his team gave a whistle,
And away they all flew
  like the down of a thistle.

But I heard him exclaim,
   ere he drove out of sight:
"Happy Christmas to all,
   and to all
      a good night!"

Happy christmas and to all a goodnight